Kangaroo Christmas

by M. E. Rose

illustrated by Bróna Keenan

BAYEUX

Bayeux Arts Inc.
Kangaroo Christmas
M.E.Rose

© 2006 Michael E. Rose

Published by:
Bayeux Arts Incorporated
119 Stratton Crescent S.W.
Calgary, Alberta, Canada T3H 1T7

Printed and bound in Canada

Library and Archives Canada Cataloguing in Publication

Rose, Michael E. (Michael Edward)
     Kangaroo Christmas / Michael E. Rose ; illustrated by
Bróna Keenan.

ISBN 1-896209-89-0

     I. Title.

PS8585.O729K36 2006   C813'.6   C2006-906012-6

The publisher gratefully acknowledges the assistance of the
Alberta Foundation for the Arts, the Canada Council for
the Arts, and the Government of Canada through the Book
Publishing Industry Development Program.

for Lucy, Juliette and Jordan

Kangaroo Christmas

It's hard to know where to begin this story, actually. It begins, in some ways, in Australia but you could say it really started at the North Pole, a very, very cold place an awfully long way from Australia. Where, exactly, the North Pole is located is another story, what adults call "another issue", but we won't try to settle that now. Most people only know anything about the North Pole at all because that is where Santa Claus lives, or, shall we say, where he lived, until some of the things I'm going tell you about started to happen. So let's just begin the story in Australia and get to the other parts later.

You probably know all there is to know about Santa Claus already. He is a very fat and jolly old man who was, many, many, many years ago — no one knows exactly when — put in charge of Christmas. He lived at the North Pole with his wife, Mrs. Claus, who was also rather fat and certainly very jolly, and with a lot of elves, who helped him make toys to give to children at Christmas, and with his reindeer, who pulled his sleigh all over the world on Christmas Eve so that Santa could deliver his toys to all good little girls and boys. You know all that already. What you don't know, I'm almost sure, because until now it has been a secret story, is that once upon a time, Santa decided that he wanted to retire.

That means he had had enough of working hard all year round in the ice and snow of the North Pole, making toys, or supervising elves making toys, and reading letters from children and replying to the letters and planning things and looking after his reindeer. And then there was the biggest job of all, each year, to travel all around the world in his giant sleigh, in all kinds of weather, delivering thousands and thousands and thousands of toys to good little girls and boys. It wasn't that he didn't enjoy the work. Of course he enjoyed it. It was just that after years and years and years and years of doing all that he simply started to get a little tired.

Mrs. Claus noticed it first, in fact. She noticed that Santa was moving a little slower while he worked and that he made fewer toys each day than he used to and that he started asking his elves to make more toys in order to keep up the level of production. The elves didn't mind, of course, because they liked their work and they did what they could, but the fact of the matter was that Santa wasn't doing everything that he used to do and one thing was leading to another and this created what adults call "a little tension" sometimes. There were small signs sometimes that Santa wasn't as happy as he could be and that maybe he needed a little rest.

No one wanted to be first to suggest that to

him, of course, because he was Santa Claus, the one and only Santa Claus, and it was up to him to decide how he wanted to organize things. But Mrs. Claus and the elves could see that he sometimes wasn't the Santa they remembered from the old days and they began to be a little worried about him. No one, however, wanted to tell him what to do. So one day, not too very long ago, not too many years ago, when he began to say that he was tired and looking for a little change, a little break from living at the frozen North Pole and making toys day after day, most of them thought this wasn't such a bad thing. They knew Santa well enough by then to be sure he wouldn't leave his duties completely, that he would make sure everything was left completely in order while he had his rest and make sure enough toys were made, and delivered, to keep all the good little boys and girls of the world excited and happy.

They were, however, very surprised when Santa looked up from his workbench one day, and pushed aside his mustaches with the back of his hand and said: "You know, I think it is time that I retired." Mrs. Claus, in fact, said: "Goodness gracious me", which, if you knew Mrs. Claus well enough, you would find an extraordinary outburst. A few of the elves dropped their tiny tools when Santa spoke, and looked at each other with worried expressions. A rest, yes, that was fine. But retirement? That was another thing entirely. They wondered how things would work, with Santa off the job. They wondered if he would ever come back to work. They wondered about who would be in charge of Christmas if Santa retired. They wondered a lot of things and most of them found it a bit hard to get on with their work that day. I think anyone would, after hearing something like that.

Well, you may be asking yourselves around now what all of this has to do with Australia. I told you that the story, the secret story, could be said to have started in Australia and the last few pages of this story have very definitely not been in Australia, but at the North Pole. Australia is a very

sunny and bright and blue-sky sort of place, and the North Pole is not like that at all. It is completely covered in snow and often dark and cloudy and very cold and people have to wear heavy coats and hats and mittens and mufflers just to keep warm. And please don't ask what a muffler is, because it will just distract us unnecessarily from the story that has to be told. Just be clear, if you can, about the big difference between Australia and the North Pole, and then you will be able to understand everything much better.

The fact is, Santa was getting older and getting tired and he wanted a break from the work and the cold and the snow and he decided that the place he wanted to go was at the exact opposite side of the world. Down Under. Australia. And Australia, as all Australian children and most adults will know, and as I suppose I have already told you, is a very warm and sunny and blue-sky sort of place and the sort of place where people like Santa Claus might decide to go if they wanted to get away from it all for a while. It is certainly as different a place from the North Pole as you could ever imagine. And, weather conditions aside, Santa had simply got to the stage of his life, the stage of what some adults would call "his career", that he wanted to do something really, really unusual.

He had often thought about Australia, on slow days when he was making toys at his workbench, what it might be like to go Down Under and to see lots of different things. He wondered about things like kangaroos and koala bears and platypuses. He wondered, actually, on some of his bad days, whether it was indeed correct to say platypuses when you were talking about more than one platypus or whether it was correct to say platypus for one or for several. That was the sort of thing he started to think about at his workbench and once you start thinking like that, after years and years and years of making toys at the North Pole, it is not so surprising that you might start to think about taking a rest and maybe even about retirement.

Of course, Santa at first kept all of this from Mrs. Claus and the elves and his reindeer, because he didn't want to alarm anyone unnecessarily. That was the kind of man he was. But after a very long time having these feelings and thinking these thoughts, he made up his mind that enough was enough. He was going to move to Australia and retire. He was going to organize things at the North Pole so that toys continued to be made and toys continued to be delivered every Christmas and he would, as adults say, "oversee things" from the other side of the world while resting in the sun under a bright blue sky.

You can see how all of this sounded rather attractive. Even Mrs. Claus, who wasn't one to complain very much, had from time to time thought of resting a little more and of getting away from the ice and snow of the North Pole. But she had never said anything about this to anyone. Now, with Santa thinking along these lines, she had to admit to herself, and to her favorite elves in whom she sometimes confided, that she found the idea rather attractive.

Of course, a big change like this doesn't happen overnight. You can't go overnight from being Santa Claus, in charge of Christmas at the North Pole, to resting on a beach in Australia. It talks a bit of planning and organization, especially if you take your responsibilities seriously and especially if you want to make sure that toys continue to get made, good toys, and that these will be delivered, on time and in perfect condition, to children all over the world on that one long and important night we call Christmas Eve.

So after Santa had made up his mind, and after he had announced his decision that important day not so very long ago, he went about the business of getting things organized properly.

He investigated various possibilities and spoke with various important and influential people and began to formulate a plan. He spoke about it to Mrs. Claus and he spoke to some of his older and more experienced elves and he sometimes even whispered bits of his plan into the ears of some of his reindeer as they munched their suppers in the reindeer barn. No one seemed to think it was a bad plan but then, to be honest, no one had had any experience of these things before and no one knew how Santa Claus, the man in charge of Christmas, should go about leaving this very important job in the hands of others. Some of the elves were, in fact, a little worried about the whole idea but they trusted Santa and knew that his intentions were good and that he needed a rest and they decided that if he came up with a plan that it would be one he had thought about for a long time and that everything would be OK. Or so they hoped. Because it was a very big change and one, as adults like to say, that was "fraught with consequences".

Anyway, here is what Santa decided to do. He decided that he would sign a contract with a very big company, with a large group of people who wore suits and ties and carried briefcases and got in and out of taxis in big cities. He decided that the contract would say that these people would look after things at the North Pole in his absence, that they would make sure that everything was OK and that toys continued to get made and elves still had their work to do and the reindeer continued to get fed and that letters from children asking for special, quite specific Christmas presents continued to get answered. And so on and so forth, as the contract actually said.

It was a very large contact with very small writing and lots of seals and ribbons and stamps all over it and most of Santa's helpers at the North Pole thought it looked very official indeed. The people who signed it on behalf of the management company also looked very official and very serious, and no one expected there would be any trouble whatsoever. None whatsoever. And in any case, part of the contract stipulated (that is an adult word for "said") that if anything bad or complicated happened or if there was any sign that production of toys or any other aspect of the Christmas operation were running into trouble, then Santa was to be informed in Australia, immediately, and he would suggest a solution. So there was no real reason to worry.

To be honest, some elves and a few of the older reindeer did worry, and Mrs. Claus started to worry a little bit herself when the contract was being drawn up and signed. And to be very, very honest, Santa Claus himself looked a little worried when he took up his old quill pen, and dipped it into his bottle of ice-blue ink to sign the document in the days before he left. He never said to anyone that he was worried, but those who knew him well could see that there were a few worry wrinkles around the wrinkles he already had, making him appear doubly wrinkled as he signed his name to the contract in the days before he left the North Pole to start a new life in Australia, managing Christmas from there, from Down Under.

Well, I suppose you could say that is Part One

of the story. I told you, if you remember, that the story began in Australia and now I have gone on for a long time telling you about the North Pole part of the story, which, in some ways, is where the story started. But really, the important part of the story begins in Australia after Santa decided to retire and leave it to others to see to the day to day work of organizing Christmas. The part in Australia is where you begin to see what really happened and what was important and what actually happened to Santa. So let's say you have now heard the beginning part of the story but the actual story, the secret and important part, begins in Australia. This part of the story has never been told before. Bits and pieces of the first part, about Santa sometimes getting tired have been told before maybe. But not this part, the Australian part.

Here's what happened.

Santa left the North Pole as planned. It was a very sad day, and many of the elves and certainly all eight of his regular reindeer, and in particular Rudolph the red-nosed reindeer, who had a tendency to be forlorn, well, they all started to cry. Santa had decided to leave the reindeer behind, if only because the climate in Australia is not right at all for reindeer who have spent all their lives in the snow and ice of the North Pole. He left all but a few of his oldest and most trusted elves behind and he even left a few of those behind, to look after the day to day work of making toys and answering letters.

He also brought with him Mrs. Claus, of course, and as he would, and he brought his Christmas sleigh. He simply could not part with that sleigh and the business people in suits assured him they would find another way of transporting toys around the world to good little girls and boys, and they assured him that no matter what means of transport they decided upon, the eight regular reindeer would be, as adults say "fully involved". Still, despite those assurances, it was a sad day for everyone concerned when Santa left the North

Pole. Santa had that doubly wrinkled worried look on his face and Mrs. Claus looked very sad indeed and the elves who were to accompany Santa to Australia carried their elfin duffel bags with no enthusiasm. True, it was an adventure to move to Australia and the weather there was certainly better than the North Pole, but no one really wants to leave familiar things, when all is said and done, and no one likes to say goodbye to friends.

The business people in suits assured everyone that the plan was a good one and that they would take care of the operation very well and that at the first sign of trouble they would contact Santa in Australia and that everyone would phone and write and send emails just as often as they liked and that everyone would be one big happy Christmas operation family just like before, except that some of them would live in Australia and some would live at the North Pole. "This is the way things are done nowadays," the business people said, and Santa nodded, somewhat hesitantly it seemed, in agreement.

Mrs. Claus wiped her eyes and the elves who were going on the trip hoisted their elfin duffle bags to their shoulders and got onto the waiting airplane and looked out the round windows at their friends and the familiar old workshop.

For, as you can imagine, Santa and his little group were going to travel to Australia by plane. Without reindeer it was impossible to pull the Christmas sleigh all the way to where they were traveling and even if their reindeer were coming along it would be wrong to use the Christmas sleigh except at Christmas. What would happen if little boys and girls looked up in the sky and saw the sleigh whizzing overheard? They could think it was Christmas and get confused and this would not be a good thing. So the sleigh was loaded onto the giant waiting airplane and the elves were all on board and Santa Claus and Mrs. Claus climbed up and waved goodbye at the door at the top of the steps.

Everyone waved and waved, even the business people in suits waved and waved. Then the door closed and the plane carrying Santa and his group whooshed up into the sky and on to their new lives in Australia. Which is where the story actually begins.

For a while, everything went very well indeed. Santa was delighted with Australia and even though it was a big life change for him and the people who had left the North Pole with him, he was, for a while, able to forget his sadness and enjoy life Down Under. He needed the rest; everyone admitted that and they could see that the rest and the sunshine and the blue sky and the Down Under way of life was doing him a lot of good. Just seeing Santa in a pair of surfer's shorts did everybody a lot of good.

Santa would get up late, later than everyone else, and have a long big breakfast. He would stand at the door to his little house on the beach, somewhere Down Under in a place called Beachside, and look out at the sand and the big blue sky and say in a very loud voice: "Ho ho ho, and not a flake of snow. No, no, no, not a flake of snow." Mrs. Claus, who would generally be out gardening or pottering around, which is what adults do when they have no real jobs to do, would hear Santa say that and she would smile, knowing he was resting and getting happier again day by day. The elves, who had learned to surf and were getting better at it by the day, could hear Santa's laughter from way out on the waves. They smiled to each other as they tumbled around in the waves and got on and off their little elfin boards and taught each other surfing techniques.

Santa would read sometimes in the mornings, or walk on the beach and say hello to local boys and girls, some of whom thought they recognized this fat old man with the bushy white beard. Some little boys and girls even said "Santa! Santa!" when they saw him coming, but their mothers and fathers would smile and say: "No, I'm afraid not, children. Santa, as every child knows, lives at the North Pole, and he certainly does not wear shorts and sunglasses." The parents actually found the old man in the shorts and sunglasses looked quite a lot like Santa Claus but they knew Santa would not be walking around in Australia looking like that so they just "put it down to coincidence", which is what adults do when they have no idea whatsoever what is going on.

Santa would just smile at the children and their parents and say nothing. His plan to retire Down Under was a secret and, in any case he did not want children to think he was not hard at work at the North Pole organizing letters and toys and reindeer transport for next Christmas. He enjoyed the attention on the beach, all the same.

Everyone missed their old friends, of course. And they missed the reindeer terribly. No one had guessed how much they would miss the reindeer. They often talked about the reindeer as they barbecued their Australian suppers at the beach and wondered how reindeer would actually feel in a hot climate near the beach, whether they might like it or not. All but one of the small group of elves and certainly Santa and Mrs. Claus were convinced it was far too hot Down Under for reindeer to live happily, and so they reassured themselves that it was a good thing to have left the reindeer back at the North Pole. But the reindeer were sorely missed.

Mrs. Claus missed the reindeer so much that she developed the idea they should assemble a herd of eight kangaroos, to keep the group in Australia company on lonely days and to remind them of home. Santa was at first not in favour of this idea. First, he said, there was nothing at all similar between reindeers and kangaroos. Second, he said, having a herd of kangaroos around the house would just remind them of the reindeer back home and make everyone feel bad. But Mrs. Claus, and some of the elves, kept on asking and kept on asking and eventually Santa agreed that they could see if any kangaroos were interested in the idea of staying around their house to keep them company when they got homesick.

Well, as you can imagine, at first the local kangaroos were a little suspicious. They didn't know what to make of this group of new Australians; a fat old man in shorts, his equally plump wife who seemed to spend her days in the garden saying "Goodness gracious me" when she spotted a new type of flower or when a kookaburra laughed at her from a gum tree. But Mrs. Claus had "a way with animals", as adults sometimes say, and slowly she was able to persuade a few kangaroos to stop hopping around aimlessly and instead to spend much of their day hanging around at the back door of the house. She had a word with some of the older, more sensible kangaroos, and told them how she hoped to assemble a little herd to make the backyard look homey, and they, being kangaroos and very easygoing about such things, agreed to help out when they could.

And so it was that one day Santa came back from his walk along the beach, carrying his sandals in one hand as he had started doing, and saw a lovely little herd of kangaroos hanging around his back door. Mrs. Claus had even found

one smallish extra kangaroo, sometimes known as a wallaby, with a quite red nose that reminded her, and eventually Santa, very much of Rudolph the red-nosed reindeer, who was used, as everyone knows, for Christmas emergencies.

The tricky part was naming them. None of the kangaroos, not one, liked the North Pole names they were expected to use. None of them could remember ever hearing names like Donder or Blitzen or Prancer or Vixen. But, as we all know, Mrs. Claus had a way with animals and eventually she persuaded eight kangaroos to take on the official North Pole reindeer names. Eventually, in fact, all members of the little kangaroo herd started to like the new situation and their new friends and their new names. Children, and even some adults, from up and down the beach, started to come over to look at the scene, with the fat old man in shorts and his wife and their odd looking group of small elfin friends and the herd of kangaroos with strange new names. Some of the adults murmured things about the changes in the neighborhood, but there was no real problem and everyone, almost everyone, just said nothing at all and let the new Australians get on with whatever it was they had come to Australia to do.

And this was the start of the problem. Because while everyone in the little group from the North Pole knew Santa needed rest and wanted to retire, none of them knew how long he would find his new life satisfying enough to stop him from worrying about how things were going back home. It took, in fact, quite a long time for this to happen. There was lots to do in Australia and there was never any snow and Santa spent many a happy day walking along the beach, smiling at local children and watching Mrs. Claus tend to her garden and the new herd of kangaroos.

But eventually, slowly but surely, Santa started to think about Christmas. That was, after all, his job for many, many, many, many years, and, as adults say, "old habits die hard". So one day, not long after breakfast and his morning walk by the sea, not long after watching his elves demonstrate their growing expertise on surfboards, Santa had a quiet word with Mrs. Claus. He said: "I wonder how things are going back up at the North Pole. I just wonder, sometimes, how all of that might be going."

He wasn't worrying. He was just wondering.

Well, back up at the North Pole, if you want to know the truth, things were not going according to plan. Not at all.

It is, in fact, a little hard to know where to begin the story of what had gone wrong. Just about everything had gone wrong; everything was changed.

There was, for example, the matter of what adults would call "working conditions" for the elves and for the reindeer. When Santa Claus was in charge of things at the North Pole, everyone worked at little tables or in small groups, putting together toys that needed to be put together, pitching in to help each other when necessary and working alone if that was better. They just got on with the job as a big happy team and somehow, each year, all of the work got done by Christmas Eve and there were enough sturdy, pretty little well-made toys to go around.

The toys were simple, of course, nothing too fancy but they were lovely little toys that all children found fun to play with and which lasted a long, long time and never broke even if you played with them a little too hard sometimes. All of these toys got made in time for Christmas when Santa was in charge of things and everyone enjoyed the work and felt proud at the end of every day.

That didn't seem to be enough for the people in suits who had signed the management contract with Santa Claus. They started, slowly at first but then faster and faster as they got more accustomed to things, to introduce a lot of changes in the way toys got made and the sort of toys that got made and what the elves could or couldn't do during their working days.

For example, they decided that a lot more

toys had to be produced each day. That meant the sturdy, little, fun and special toys that Santa's helpers used to make, in wood most of the time or in soft fabrics or other nice materials, were being made less and less. "Times are changing," the people in suits said when anyone ever complained. "We have to move with the times; children are not the same as they used to be." Well, the elves simply knew this was not correct, and that children were always the same and always like sturdy, little, fun and special toys, but the people in suits saw things differently and insisted that the elves start to make very complicated and difficult toys with lots of plastic bits that broke off easily or that hurt when they rubbed up against your skin or that had really difficult instruction manuals that fathers and mothers had to read before you could put them together to use for having fun. Some of them even needed batteries before they could be used at all. So there was a good deal of dissatisfaction among the elves about these changes.

Things got even worse when the new managers started installing machines to help produce things even faster. The new managers said the elves were working too slowly and that the machines would help them make things faster and faster, so more toys could be ready more quickly for Christmas. The elves, or some of their braver representatives, argued that children didn't really need lots and lots of toys to be happy. Just a few toys accumulated over the years would satisfy most good little girls and boys, especially if the toys were solid and brightly coloured and lots of fun to play with. And especially if it was something they very much wanted to get for Christmas, something they had hoped and hoped and hoped they might get under the Christmas tree and which would be handed to them wrapped up all nice and perfect, with a mother or a father or a sister or a brother or a friend saying: "Here is your Christmas present for this year, dearest one. I very much hope you like it."

The elves argued that this was really all that

most children needed when all was said and done, but the people in suits saw things quite a lot differently than that and so they speeded things up and changed the elves working conditions and everyone grew more and more tired and sad about the way they had to spend their days. "Santa simply would not stand for this," one brave elf said aloud one day from his place beside a huge clanking toy machine, where he worked long hours wearing ear protectors that really didn't protect his ears at all. He was lucky the workshop was so noisy that the new managers didn't hear him. Otherwise, he might have been sent off, probably without his lunch.

Lunch was another sore point with the elves. When Santa Claus and Mrs. Claus were around, lunch was a festive affair. When some of the elves started to get hungry after working for a few hours at their toy-making tables, one or more of them might say: "What about a bit of lunch?" That would get others thinking about lunch and then someone would notice delicious smells coming from the big old kitchen where Mrs. Claus used to spend much of her day, and Santa, too, when he saw that he needed to pitch in with cooking and cleaning duties just to do his fair share. Those cooking smells inevitably meant that lunch was almost ready and soon the whole happy group of elves would sit around a seemingly endless long table, eating plates of hot and cold tasties, with hot and cold delicious drinks and then lots of wonderful tasting sweet little morsels for dessert. They would rest a bit afterward and tell stories or listen to Mr. and Mrs. Claus talking quietly to each other as they cleaned up and then the elves would move back to work to finish their tasks for the day.

It was like that for years and years, and everyone liked it just so. But the new managers who took over after Santa retired and moved to Australia changed even that part of the elves' working lives. Lunch was to be half an hour only, after a bell rang. The elves were expected to line up at a sandwich machine, that would cough out triangle sandwiches in a triangular plastic box after they put coins into as slot that was too high for most of them to reach comfortably anyway. The sandwiches looked old and had funny-coloured bits pushed inside and the bread seemed hard and dry. They had to drink water with their sandwiches, standing near the sandwich machine and then they had to get right back to work, with no time to talk and exchange views on the events of the day. The elves did not like this change in their working lives very much at all.

But what was worst, probably, in a series of bad things, was the singing rule. Or rather, the new rule against singing. You see, when Santa was in charge of things at the North Pole, the elves would almost always sing as they worked. Not always, but almost always. It usually began when one elf started to hum a little tune as he worked on a nice sturdy toy. Then another elf would join in and hum along. Another might start to tap his foot or snap his fingers and then someone would inevitably "burst into song", which is what adults say when someone starts to sing. Then it was an all-out singsong, loud and long, and it make the work day go by just like magic.

Sometimes even Santa himself would join in the singing, even though his voice was very, very low and it made some of the elves laugh as they sang. Laughing and singing at the same time, as most of you will already know, is very hard to do and does not allow for the best quality singing. But everyone had fun, even Santa, and no one liked it to stop.

Well, the new managers at the North Pole didn't like it when people sang as they worked and they really didn't like it when elves or anyone else sang and laughed at the same time. So they established the No Singing Rule. This, to state it as simply as possible, meant that no one was allowed to sing as they worked. The new managers said that singing was a distraction, a sign that elves were not concentrating completely on their work. They also said that with heavy machinery around, it was not safe to sing. No one could quite understand why singing beside a big ugly toy machine was not safe, but the rule was established anyway and then all you could hear at the North Pole on any given work day was the clank of big toy-making machines and the clinkety-clink at lunch time of elfin coins dropping into big sandwich machines that coughed out triangle sandwiches in triangular plastic boxes.

Did I say that the lunch situation was the worst thing? Maybe I made a mistake. Maybe the worst thing was the letters problem. Yes, this was probably the worst thing, at least as far as it concerned all the little children of the world. It certainly upset the elves, who were already very upset about the No Singing Rule and the lunch situation and a lot of other things. The letters problem was this: the people in suits who had signed the management contract with Santa Claus had not kept their promise to look after all of the thousands and millions of letters which children send every year to Santa Claus at the North Pole with requests for specific toys.

This tradition goes back many, many, many, many years. No one knows how it started but it was certainly part of the Christmas tradition and every little boy or girl who wrote a letter to Santa was confident that it would get to the North Pole somehow and, more importantly, be read by him and/or one of his helper elves, filed carefully away and the requests for toys entered into the Official Toys Ledger (ledger being another name for a big and important book) and consulted when the North Pole elves were making toys for delivery at Christmas. These letters were very important to everyone and treated accordingly. But once Santa retired, the letters were not treated as important anymore.

Well, that is not quite true. The elves treated them as important but the people in suits interfered with that, and made up new rules and procedures for dealing with the letters, and took the responsibility for reading and recording toy requests away from the elves and gave it to smaller, assistant people in suits who carried the letters away to a dim room with a sign on it that said: "Unsolicited Correspondence". They assured the elves that the letters would be dealt with in that room, but no one explained exactly what was done with them and no one saw any of the people in suits or any of the smaller assistant people in suits actually filling in the Official Toys Ledger and it all got quite out of hand.

Some of the elves became suspicious and the most suspicious of them even said that the letters were simply not being read at all. But that would be such a terrible thing to do with children's letters that most elves just wouldn't let themselves think that and "hoped for the best", which is what adults say when they are desperately worried about something but have no idea whatsoever what to do about it. So the letters problem was just not dealt with at all.

No one knew quite what to do about any of the big problems that were developing. So, after weeks and weeks and weeks of unhappiness, some of the elves began to whisper to each other that perhaps they had better let Santa Claus know what was going on.

Well, that was easier said than done. Because in addition to the No Singing Rule and a lot of other rules at the North Pole, there was the No Telephoning Anyone rule and the No Calling Santa Claus In Particular rule. You'll remember, of course, that before leaving for Australia Santa had told everyone, including the people in suits, that if any problem arose anyone one could call him at any time for help and advice. The people in suits had nodded politely at this and had promised that this would be the way things worked. But now, when there were very serious problems indeed at the North Pole, they, as adults would say, "reneged" on their promise.

Whenever an elf tried to pick up the telephone to dial Australia, a supervisor in a suit would come running up, take the receiver and place it back saying: "No calls. None at all." And that was that.

The elves had no telephones of their own,

only the ones in the toy workshop, so they were, you could say, a bit stuck. Letters were another problem. They couldn't be seen to be writing letters while they were supposed to be making toys and even if they tried to send off a letter they had written in their beds at night, a supervisor in a suit would say "Oh very well, I'll mail that for you", but then would secretly tear it up into hundreds of tiny pieces and dispose of it when the elves were busy making toys or lining up for triangle sandwiches. The elves knew their letters were not getting through, because Santa Claus never called and never came. They, quite frankly, didn't know what to do.

Then one day, a very resourceful elf named Squeaker — no one knew how he had got that name — wrote a very long and angry letter to Santa Claus late one night when all of the elves and the reindeer and the people in suits were asleep. The letter told Santa exactly what was going wrong, what changes had been made, how unhappy everyone was and how much they needed his help and advice. Then he folded it up into a very sleek paper airplane, wrote on its side: "Urgent. Urgent. Air Mail for Santa Claus. Beachside, Australia".

Squeaker waited alone at his window until he heard a great freezing gust of North Pole wind blow past, and then he quickly opened the glass and launched the plane into the clear night air. The north wind took the little aircraft up, up and up into the night sky and carried it for hundreds and thousands of miles southward, towards the warmer part of the world, where the sky was blue and the sun shone every day. How, exactly, the paper airplane with the urgent message actually got into Santa's hands on the beach on Australia is what adults call "one of life's little mysteries", which is what adults say when they are not quite sure how something happened. But happen it did, with a little help along the way from good people who knew just by looking at the word Urgent on the side that this message was critically important and must be delivered.

One day, then, many days after the launch of the urgent airmail letter, Santa Claus was coming back from his daily stroll along the beach when he saw a small crowd of elves and their new local friends and Mrs. Claus gathered by the mailbox at the front gate of his house. They were examining something that looked like a very battered paper airplane, covered in spots and stains and very much worse for the wear. Everyone was pointing at the word Urgent on the side, and the return address which read "Santa's Workshop, North Pole". There was quite a commotion. No one had opened up the paper plane, because it was after all addressed to Santa. But everyone had a feeling it contained important information.

When Santa had sat down on a bench beside the gate and when someone had run for his wire-rimmed spectacles, another word for eyeglasses, he began to read the letter, very slowly so he would not miss a word. He read it slowly, then he looked up at his friends who were gathered around him watching him read, and then he read the letter all over again. No one said a word. Then all of a sudden Santa sprang up off the bench and shouted so loudly that a nearby flock of parrots fluttered in shock up into the air. "This is preposterous! This is outrageous! This cannot be happening at the North Pole!" he shouted at the top of his voice.

Santa's face became so red that Mrs. Claus rushed into the house to get a damp cloth to put over his forehead. Santa lay down on the bench, breathing in and out like a big toy steam engine and Mrs. Claus cooled his forehead. "There, there, Santa," she said. "It can't be as bad as all that."

"Bad?" Santa bellowed. "Bad? It is worse than bad. It is positively preposterous!"

No one dared to say a word. No one had ever seen Santa quite like this before. They all knew something terrible had happened but no one dared ask Santa anything else while he was in such a state. They waited, and they watched, and they knew that eventually Santa would tell them all what was going on back home.

Well, that, I suppose, is the end of another part of the story. I can't remember if that would be Part Two or Part Three but it certainly does feel like the end of another part of the story. What happens next, of course, is critically important and, as the adults say "fraught with consequences". I suppose it would be best if I simply got on with the next part of the story and told you what happened next. But be warned. The story becomes very worrying and very exciting around now, and you should prepare yourselves as best you can because the problem with stories like this is you just never know how they are going to end, how things will all turn out. Stories like this can go any which way, really, and you just never know how things will all turn out.

Santa had had a nasty shock. It took him a while to regain his composure and tell everyone what Squeaker the elf had told him in the letter. Eventually, however, Santa told them all about the nasty changes that had been made back home at the North Pole and everyone, even some of the local people who stood listening, and certainly all of the kangaroos, had been, as they say, "profoundly shocked". Appalled, even. Mrs. Claus wiped a tear from her eye; that was how upsetting the news was for her.

There was no doubt in anyone's mind, however, that Santa would take the situation immediately in hand. They knew he would do something, immediately. Because he was, after all, still in charge of Christmas, even though he was retired and he would not stand by to see such changes made at the North Pole.

Santa told them all the story and they all listened carefully and then he sat on his bench for what seemed a very long time. He wiped his mustaches with the back of his hand and seemed on several occasions about to speak again. But he said nothing at all for a very long time. Eventually, he seemed to make up his mind about something. He stood up, scattering a few parrots and kookaburras who had perched on the back of the bench to observe the situation, and he said in a loud voice: "Mrs. Claus, could you please get me my satchel bag and a few changes of clothes. I am off to the North Pole!"

Everyone cheered, for they knew that this was exactly what must be done. "Hurray!" they all shouted. "Hurray!"

Well, as you know, once a decision like this is made in stories, things begin to move very quickly. Santa made urgent arrangements to travel to the North Pole. He would take the fastest airplane possible, by the most direct route possible, and hoped to be there in a very few days time. He decided he would go alone. He said that this would give him what adults call "moral authority". He told Mrs. Claus, who wanted to go with him, that it would be best if he settled this alone. The decision to retire and leave the Christmas workshop in the hands of others was his alone, he said, and he wanted to travel back to the North Pole alone to make things right. He was, he said, confident he could do this and promised to be back as soon as possible, carrying with him good news. He promised them all he would see to it that the situation, and above all the working conditions, at the North Pole were changed back to the way they had been before, to the way they had always been and must always be.

"Hurray!" everyone in Beachside shouted. "Hurray, and hurry back!"

Well, the truth of the matter was that Santa Claus was very worried indeed. He had that doubly wrinkled expression on his face, which was a clear sign of worry where Santa Claus was concerned. He did not, if the truth were told, know exactly what he would be able to do when he got back to the North Pole and he thought, in his heart of hearts, that the situation was very grave indeed. If things got very bad, he simply did not want Mrs. Claus and his friends to be caught up in any unpleasantness. So he decided he would go home alone, by airplane, and see what, if anything, he could do.

Well, we are right in the middle of the story now, and things look very bad. I would suggest that anybody reading this or listening and who does not know if they can deal with the extreme tension and scariness of the next few bits of the story should perhaps just stop reading or listening and not continue. Others who can manage it had better get ready for an extremely important and particularly worrisome part of the story, which is going to begin right now.

Because, you see, Santa's trip to the North Pole to fix things didn't go very well at all. Not at all. It started off badly and it got worse after that. As an example of how it went, Santa missed his airplane connections whenever he had a connection to make. Airplane connections, and missing them, is what adults talk about when they talk about traveling. They talk about that and something called "lost luggage", which is another bad thing that happens when you are traveling. And you know there is a lot of traveling to do if you are going from Australia to the North Pole.

So there were missed connections of all sorts, and lost luggage, and a lot of other nasty things all along the way. But that was not the worst thing; far from it.

When Santa finally got to the North Pole and to the gates of the big place where his workshop and house and elves' houses and other buildings all stood, he was absolutely stupefied (there is a good word for you to know) at what he saw. It was snowing, and a bit dark, but he could see clearly that there were now guards outside the gate, with black uniforms and peaked caps and grim expressions on their faces. There were signs on the gate that said things like "No Trespassing, Not Ever. Offenders will Be Yelled At". Another sign said "No Visitors, Not Ever. Especially No Visitors for Elves". It was all very nasty and scary.

When the guards saw Santa trudging up the snowy road to the gates, they didn't quite know what to do. He was easily recognizable, as one of the most famous people in the world, and even though he had a nice tan from all of the

Australian sunlight and even though he had lost a little weight, it was easy to recognize him. He had put on his usual red suit, for example, because no one ever wears Australian surfer shorts at the North Pole, and he had put on his usual red Santa Claus hat, so no one was in any doubt whatsoever that it was Santa Claus trudging purposefully down the snowy road to the gates that afternoon when he arrived back at the North Pole.

The guards, of course, were very, very surprised to see him and looked at each other nervously, not knowing quite what to do. Normally they would have yelled meanly at any trespassers and scared them away, but this was, after all, Santa Claus who was, or had been, in charge of everything for many years. The guards knew that he had gone away and they knew that the people in suits were now in charge but they didn't know much about the exact "terms of the management contract", as the adults say, so they didn't know whether he could come in or whether he should be made to stay outside. They looked at each other, and they looked down the road and they did what any guard would do under the circumstances, whether they are nice guards or mean guards. They called their supervisors and made them decide.

Santa came up to the gate just as the guards were calling their supervisors on the emergency telephone. He was hot from all the walking he had just done to get from the road to the gate, even though the weather at the North Pole was cold that day. He was hot and not very happy after his long trip and after seeing that even at the front gate of his own place there were changes he didn't like very much. When he was in charge, people could not simply walk in to the toy workshop or to Santa's house or the elves houses, but the very few visitors who did arrive were greeted properly and asked inside and allowed to have a look around the places where secret toy making activities were not going on.

Visitors used to be encouraged to look at the not-secret parts of the toy-making operation and sometimes they were even invited to stay for lunch. But under the new management at the North Pole, all of that was changed. The job of the new guards was to make sure no one came inside, ever. And that was that. Except that no one had anticipated a situation like this, with Santa Claus himself coming up to the gate and wanting to be let inside.

The supervisors were a little worried too. They hadn't anticipated this either. So when they came down to the gate and saw Santa standing there they didn't know what to say. Santa, however, knew what to say and he said it in a very loud voice. He said: "This is positively preposterous!" He said it so loud that everyone inside the walls heard it and heard it echo a few times off the walls of the workshop building and Santa's house and the elves houses and the big barn where Santa's sleigh used to be parked. The reindeers heard it and the elves heard it and everyone, even the most senior people in suits, knew that Santa was back and not very happy at all.

At the gates, there was what adults like to call "a tense standoff". Santa stood staring angrily at the guards and saying occasionally: "This is positively preposterous! I am not being allowed into my own workshop and home. This is preposterous!" The guards, or those among them who dared say anything at all, and the supervisors who dared to say anything at all, said: "So sorry, Santa. No visitors, no exceptions. Those are the rules. Those are our instructions."

Santa Claus demanded to speak to the person in charge. He demanded to see that person right away. But of course there were delays. Guards and supervisors rushed to and fro, making calls on emergency phones while Santa waited angrily outside the gate of his own workshop and home, with snowflakes gathering on his shoulders and catching in his bushy eyebrows and generally making him look more and more like Santa by the minute. There was a great deal of rushing around and lots of phoning and whispered consultations and then, after what seemed like a very long time, a group of quite official-looking people in suits came to the gate. They carried briefcases and mobile telephones and looked very official indeed. They stood at the gate, and eventually one of them said to Santa: "What seems to be the problem?"

This sent Santa into a rage. His face got even redder under his Australian tan. His eyes grew wider than they already were and his wrinkles deepened alarmingly. He breathed in and out like a big toy steam engine and he waved his hands in the air. "The problem?" he said. "The problem? The problem is that this is all positively preposterous! I am Santa Claus, this is the North Pole, and I am here to see what on earth is going on. And I am not being allowed into my own workshop and home. That is the problem. That is precisely the preposterous problem, and I will not stand for it for a minute longer!"

By now, a crowd of elves and most of the reindeer had come down to the other side of the gate, despite this being strictly against the rules.

All toy making work had stopped. Everyone heard about the tense standoff at the gate and everyone hurried down to the entrance to see what was going to happen. Some elves called out to Santa from a long way away, where guards were keeping them back. "Hurray!" they called out. "You're back, you're back at last. Come in! Come in, come in."

One brave elf even called out in a loud voice: "Santa, please, hurry back in, they've changed everything, everything is changed. Even lunch is changed!" Guards pushed that brave elf down onto the snow and stared at him with very mean looks and he, perhaps wisely, decide he should probably not say anything more. He sat in the wet snow looking scared and worried but also with the look of someone who had done the right thing. His elfin friends all applauded and congratulated him until guards stared meanly at them too, and made them stop.

Santa was arguing with the guards and the people in suits. "I want to see the person in charge!" he bellowed. "Bring me to the person in charge!" But it was no use. The people in suits said they could not do that because no one person was actually in charge. The North Pole and the toy workshop and everything else was being run by what adults call "a Board". No one person was in charge, so no one could actually be said to be to blame for anything bad that happened. The group of people in suits would, they said, take Santa's complaints to the Board if he wanted them to do that and they would, as adults say, "get back to him as soon as possible". But there was nothing they could do that day, nothing at all.

Santa was enraged again. He said: "I have reliable information that everything here has been changed. I am told that my elves are working much harder than they have ever worked to make toys that are not right, not right at all. I'm told that there are machines now to make toys as well. I am told that there are changes in the lunch situation, that there is no singing for the elves as they work, that everything, positively everything, is changed and for the worse. I am told that even the letters from children all round the world are being ignored, completely ignored. And I will not stand for this. Do you hear? I am Santa Claus, and I will not stand for this. Let me inside and let me see for myself what is going on in there. I demand to be let inside!"

The elves and the reindeer all cheered and clapped. The guards looked nervous and moved closer to Santa in a very menacing way. They looked over to the people in suits, waiting for their instructions. It was a very tense situation indeed. No one knew what was going to happen next.

Well, here is what happened. One of the people in suits said in a loud clear voice: "We're closed." He signaled for the other people in suits to come back inside. He signaled for the guards to come back inside. And he signaled for the giant gates to be swung shut. Santa saw what was going to happen and he pushed forward trying to get past the guards, but they pushed him roughly back and they pushed him away from the gates and then they darted inside and all pushed the giant gates shut with a terrifically loud bang. The elves and reindeers inside all started to shout and some of them even started to cry, despite the weather being far too cold for this. The tears froze painfully on their cheeks before they could hit the ground. Many of the elves were crying and others were shouting and it was a terrible scene, a really terrible scene.

None of the elves and reindeer could believe what had just happened. Santa Claus, the man in charge of Christmas, had been refused entry to his own workshop and home. He had been treated very meanly indeed by the guards and the people in suits and the gate had been slammed very rudely in his face. No one could believe what they had seen. Everyone had thought Santa would come back eventually to help them. Everyone had thought he would arrive and tell the people in charge that none of the changes they had made were acceptable and that things would get back to normal with no more trouble than that. But they had been mistaken. They could see now that the situation was bad, very bad, and they were not sure what they should do next.

So they allowed themselves to be pushed back to their work places and they put on their ear protectors and tried to get on with their work, because Christmas was coming and there were lots of toys still to be made and lots of children depending on them so they got back to their work places, and wiped their eyes and tried to get on with their jobs. But the situation was very bad indeed.

For Santa, things were as bad as they can be. At first he just stood outside the gates, looking shocked. His face showed it. He simply could not believe what had happened. He had come all the way from Australia to the North Pole and he had had the gates to his own workshop and home slammed very rudely in his face. No one had listened to him, His elves and reindeer had called out to him for help and some of them had been crying and he had been able to do nothing whatsoever about it.

Santa was so shocked and so sad and so perplexed that he sat down suddenly on the snow. He sat there and he stared at the giant gates and, for a minute, it looked like he might start to cry. But he did not cry. He was Santa Claus and he had important business to attend to and he did not have time to cry. But for a minute, it really looked like he might start.

He sat for a long time in the snow, looking at the workshop gates and the high wall that surrounded the building and houses and barns and other buildings he had been in charge of for so long. He thought about his idea to retire and move to Australia. He thought about his wife and his elfin friends waiting for him back at the beach. He thought about how they were depending on him to make things right, just as the elves and reindeer inside were depending on him to make things right. He thought and thought and thought, until the piles of snow on his shoulders and eyebrows started to get very big. Then he picked himself up, brushed himself off and said, in a very quiet voice this time: "Preposterous! Preposterous! Preposterous!"

He walked slowly around the edge of the walls, trying to decide what to do next. He walked all around to the far side, looking as sad and worried as ever he had ever looked. He trudged through the snow, in the dark and the cold, and tried to think what could be done next. Sometimes he stopped to listen, to try to hear what was going on inside, but all he could hear was the north wind and the far-off clank and hum of the new toy-making machinery the people in suits had installed inside. He kept walking and thinking until he reached the very back of the workshop grounds. And then he saw something that made him so sad, and so mad, that he almost sat down again right there in the snow.

Because piled up against the back wall of the workshop, in bins and boxes and bags, were hundreds of thousands, if not millions, of letters.

Letters from all over the world, with odd stamps on them and addressed in the shaky handwriting that children use when they write letters to Santa Claus. The letters to Santa were not just being ignored. The letters were being thrown away. Not filed for reading later. Not sent back to the children who wrote them But thrown away, in bins and boxes and bags.

Santa simply could not believe what he was seeing. Things had been very bad so far, very bad. But this was too much. To see the hundreds of thousands, if not millions, of letters sitting there in bins and boxes and bags, getting wet or blown around by the cold north wind was simply too much. Things could not get any worse than this.

But sometimes when things get very bad, something important happens to people. And that is what happened to Santa as he stood there looking at the discarded letters from children over the world. What happened was that he decided that no matter how bad things were, no matter what mistakes he had made and no matter how difficult things were going to get, he was going to make things right. He would go back to Australia as quickly as he could. He would talk to his friends back there at the beach, and he would even talk to the new friends he had met while he was in Australia and he would come up with a plan and he would return to the North Pole and make things right.

He made a promise to himself and to his elves and friends and to children all over the world that he would come back to the North Pole and make things right. He stood up as straight as he could and he leaned his head back and he raised his hands to the sides of his mouth and he shouted as loud as he possibly could: "I will be back! Just wait! All of you wait! I will be back!" The words rose up high and loud in the cold air and up over the walls and Santa knew that people inside would hear what he had shouted and knew that they would be reassured that everything was going to be alright again one day.

Santa shouted again and again in the loudest

possible voice and then he turned and starting walking as fast as he could the way he had come. He was in a hurry now, and there was no time to lose.

Well, even if you are in a hurry, you can't travel from the North Pole to Australia right away. It's a very long distance and many things can happen along the way and there is always the problem of missed connections and lost luggage. But Santa made it back to Australia as fast as he possibly could.

Mrs. Claus, of course, and the few elves who had come to Australia, and the kangaroos and the kookaburras and platypuses and koalas and some of the other Australians who had became friends with the people from the North Pole were all waiting anxiously for Santa to come back. The new friends had been told a little about what was going on and they had promised not to tell anyone else, so Mrs. Claus and the elves had at least some support as they waited for news from the North Pole. When no news came, they all got quite worried but they didn't allow themselves to think anything had gone wrong. Everything will turn out just right," they all said to each other when the worries started. "Santa Claus is going to be back soon with good news."

But some of them worried more than others and some of those really worried ones worried that things had not gone right at all. They thought that if the news was going to be good they would have heard something by now. But there was no way of telling just what was going on until Santa actually got back.

One bright, blue-sky Australian morning, when the elves were surfing and the kangaroos were hanging around the back door of the house, Santa appeared at the far end of the beach. One of the elves spotted him from far off and fell off his surfboard trying to wave and alert the others that Santa Claus had come home. Everyone ran down to the beach and started running or flying or hopping across the sand to greet him. But anyone could see that there was something terribly, terribly wrong.

For one thing, Santa had not even bothered to take off his red Santa suit, despite the hot Australian weather. Everybody had got used to him wearing shorts and sunglasses at the beach, so they were quite surprised to see him in his Santa suit. It was all rumpled and dirty and he was very hot in it and looked very red in the face and tired. It was lucky that his luggage had been lost, because he would have probably been too tired to carry it along the beach toward his house that day.

Everybody, all the elves and the kangaroos and the kookaburras and the koalas and the parrots and the platypuses and the local people who had become new friends all gathered in a big circle around Santa on the sand and waited for him to give his news. They stood there, but no one dared say a word. Santa looked so tired and so hot and so sad that no one dared say a word, not even Mrs. Claus, who stood a little outside the circle of people and elves and animals and waited for Santa to say something. Anything.

Eventually, Santa said: "There is trouble, bad trouble, at the North Pole." His friends all gasped and looked at each other and didn't know what to say. Santa said: "We have trouble on our hands, my friends. Bad trouble, the worst kind of trouble. But we are going to make things right!"

"Hurray for Santa!" said one of the elves, an optimistic fellow. But no one else said anything at all. They knew that if Santa had come all the way back from the North Pole, looking like he was looking and saying what he was saying, that the trouble must be very bad indeed.

Santa carried on walking over to Mrs. Claus, and gave her a nice big hug and a kiss. Then they walked together to their house and went inside and closed the door. Everyone else waited politely outside for a while and then went on about their daily business. They knew that Santa needed a rest and to talk privately with Mrs. Claus before he gave them any more news that day. They were all very eager to hear the whole story, but they knew that sometimes you just have to wait.

Let's see now, where are we with this story? Let's just take stock for a minute here. I suppose we are more than halfway through, well over halfway through. And it's true that things don't look very good just at this moment, at this point in the story. But you'll remember that Santa made a promise on that very bad day up at the North Pole that he would make things right. So now the rest of the story will have to be about whether he was able to do that and if so, how.

Some of you may have a bit of an idea what he decides to do at this point in the story, and some of you may not. But that is the whole point of stories, isn't it? You don't know how things are going to turn out and you read or you listen until you find out. That's what makes stories, stories, isn't it? So let's find out what happens next.

Santa first of all had a very good rest. He took off his rumpled and dirty Santa suit and had a nice bath. He slept for hours and hours and hours. When he woke up again he got into his favourite surfer shorts and had a cup of tea and sat out in the back garden with a pad of writing paper and his old quill pen and started to make a long list. At the top of the list he wrote: "Plan A". He wrote and thought and wrote for a long time, and he talked to Mrs. Claus from time to time and he developed his plan as carefully as anything he had ever done. And then, when his plan was finished, he stood up and said: "Let's have a very important meeting to talk about what must be done."

Mrs. Claus hurried outside and called everyone together. There were lots of people and animals to get together but she did it as fast as she could. Everyone sat in a big semicircle on the beach. Some of the kookaburras sat in trees. The parrots preferred to hover around and listen from the air. But everyone had been waiting for this moment and no one wanted to miss a word Santa was going to say.

When he came out of the house, Santa looked rested, but very, very serious. He walked straight over to where everyone was waiting and said: "My friends, we have bad trouble at the North Pole, as you know. The trouble is bad but I intend to make things right. And I want all of you to help me. I have a plan."

Everyone cheered. That was exactly what they hoped Santa was going to say. They waited, and he started to talk. He told them everything, even the bad bits and the sad bits and he didn't leave anything out. He told them how things had been changed at the North Pole, about how the elves were working under very bad conditions, how the people in suits had reneged on their promises and contractual obligations and their other obligations. He told them about the No Singing Rule and the new lunch arrangements and he even told them what was happening to the letters from children all over the world.

The news about the letters disturbed everyone very badly. Almost more than anything else. When Santa told them about the letters, some of the elves jumped up from the sand and shouted: "No! Impossible!" But Santa raised up his hand and asked for calm. "We will make this right," he said in a low, slow voice. "We will make this right. I have a plan."

Santa started to tell them about his plan, and the more he told them about it the more everyone started to feel a little better. It was an excellent plan, an elaborate, excellent plan and all but the most gloomy of those listening felt sure that it would work. They knew it would take a lot of effort and preparations but they knew that it would work.

Santa had decided that they would go, all of them — himself, Mrs. Claus, the elves, the kangaroos, the kookaburras and koalas and platypuses, and any of the local Australian people who wanted to come along to help — all of them would go to the North Pole together and make things right. He had thought about this all the way from the North Pole to Australia and he was confident his plan would work.

First, they would have what adults like to call "the element of surprise". None of the people in suits or the guards at the North Pole would ever expect him to come back, and certainly not with a large contingent of helpers and supporters and volunteers. And, second, Santa and his friends would arrive not as he had done the last time, up the road to the front gate of the North Pole workshop, but by air. And not by airplane, but — and this was the wonderful part of Santa's plan that everyone cheered and applauded when they heard it for the first time — in his Christmas sleigh, coming in fast and steep from the air, over the walls and into the workshop area where they would join up with the elves and the reindeer and take the place over and make things right.

The idea of whizzing in over the walls of the North Pole workshop in Santa's Christmas sleigh was a wonderful, exciting prospect to everyone. They imagined themselves all bundled into the sleigh, with perhaps the parrots and kookaburras flying in formation alongside, and maybe extra people hanging onto the runners of the sleigh or in the cargo space at the back or wherever they could find room. But some of them immediately had a question. They were reluctant to ask it, lest they be accused of looking on the dark side of things, but they felt they had to ask it anyway.

That is all very well, they said to Santa. The plan sounded just fine, as far as it went, and the idea of whizzing in over the walls of the North Pole workshop in Santa's Christmas sleigh was a wonderful, exciting prospect to everyone. But there was one big problem. The reindeer, whose job it was to pull the sleigh and who were the only ones who knew how to do that important job, were back at the North Pole, in trouble along with everyone else. How could Santa use the sleigh without his eight regular reindeer?

Santa smiled. He had expected the question and knew exactly how he would answer it. He smiled again and he walked slowly around to the back of the crowd to where his herd of kangaroos was hanging around, listening to the discussion. Santa walked over to the kangaroos and said to everyone: "My friends, I told you I had a plan. You have heard most of my plan now and there is one last part of it you have to know. These kangaroos here, good friends of ours by now and aware of the serious problems at back home, will take the place of my reindeer and pull my sleigh to the North Pole."

The kangaroos were startled. Kangaroos are easily startled, but this was very startling news indeed. One of them, in fact, was so startled he tried to hop away down the beach as fast as he could but an elf ran off to stop him. The other kangaroos looked at each other in alarm, scratching themselves with their paws and twitching their noses and putting on worried kangaroo looks. They were not sure they liked what they had just heard.

Kangaroos are very agreeable creatures, with simple hopes and dreams, and they try as much as they can to get along with everyone but, really, the thing they were best at was hopping around or hanging around at people's back doors. Not flying. And certainly not pulling a Christmas sleigh all the way from Australia to the North

Pole. Through the air, probably at night and probably, very probably, through cold night air. Kangaroos are not used to flying, they are not used to the cold and they are certainly not used to having adventures. Hopping around and hanging around is one thing, or maybe two things. But flying on dangerous adventures through cold night air was quite another.

Santa knew the kangaroos would be alarmed. He said to them: "My friends, there is nothing to be afraid of. Nothing whatsoever. I will teach you how to fly and how to pull my sleigh. We will make sure you know how it is done before we go, and we will not leave a minute, or even a second, before that."

Santa looked around at everyone and said: "Well, that is my plan. Let's get on with it."

At this point, everyone, with the possible exception of the kangaroos, felt confident the plan would work. They had the element of surprise and they believed that once they were inside the North Pole workshop they could take things over again and make things right. They would take things over again, and work very, very hard alongside those already there to get all the toys, the proper toys, ready for Christmas., They would have to read all of the letters very fast and work very hard and very fast but they were sure that they could do the job. The only small difficulty would be to get there, using Santa's sleigh and eight somewhat reluctant kangaroos.

Everyone knew what they had to do. Some of them started studying toy making handbooks. Others looked at maps. Some started making lunches, perhaps a little too early but it was something they felt they had to do. Santa's job, however, was the hardest. It was his job to teach the kangaroos how to fly and how to pull a giant Christmas sleigh. And they had very little time to learn. The lessons started the very next day.

Well, you might say Santa had his work cut out for him. Kangaroos, nice animals that they are, cannot be said to be natural fliers. Santa knew this. He also knew, from his brief but extremely happy time in Australia, that kangaroos are not the most energetic of animals. They do not exactly like new challenges. They prefer hopping and hanging around, as we have seen already in this story. So Santa decided he would have to use what adults would call his "powers of persuasion".

He called a meeting, for himself and the kangaroos. Others were not invited to attend. He stood on the beach with a blackboard and some chalk, and the kangaroos hung around in front of the board, twitching their noses and making soft kangaroo sounds as they watched and listened.

Santa drew them a fairly accurate diagram of the Christmas sleigh and its harness, which was usually used just for reindeer. He explained that with some modification to the harness, kangaroos could quite conceivably pull the sleigh all the way from Australia to the North Pole at very high altitude and in freezing cold weather and in darkness. Needless to say, the kangaroos were not immediately convinced. They examined the diagram, they looked at each other and twitched

their noses nervously and looked at the diagram again.

None of them said a word, because, as you know, kangaroos don't speak. They just make soft little kangaroos sounds. They looked at Santa's giant Christmas sleigh pulled up in the sand near-by and they looked at the elves and local tradesmen who were adapting the reindeer harnesses into a kangaroo harnesses and they said nothing. But they were nervous. Anyone could see that.

Santa said: "Right. So that's all reasonably clear, I would imagine. Let's have a try. We are going to have a practice run."

The kangaroos reluctantly got into position. Everyone helped get them into their harnesses and once they were rigged up, everyone stood back to see what it looked like. A local man, a Beachsider, stood in his wide Australian-looking hat and his big baggy shorts and sunglasses and said, somewhat dubiously to Santa: "And where do yer think yer goin' in that contraption, mate?"

Santa, not one to be discouraged by unsolicited critical remarks from strangers, said simply: "We're off to the North Pole." The Beachsider said: "Fair dinkum? That's in Canada isn't it, mate?" Santa simply said: "Close enough." He knew that his planned expedition to the North Pole to save Christmas from the people in suits had become something of an open secret in the little community of Beachside and he knew the locals were a discreet lot, not prone to idle gossip that could put the plan in danger, but he thought it best to say as little as possible to people not actually in his group, if only to maintain the element of surprise.

Well, the first flight of the Christmas sleigh, I can now reveal, was not a success. Despite Santa's careful explanation of aerodynamics, which is an adult word for explaining how big heavy things, which have no business in the air, can actually fly from one place to another, and despite his careful drawing of diagrams and his explanation of the difference between "striding", which is what reindeers do when they pull a Christmas sleigh, and "hopping", which is what kangaroos do for no particular reason at all, the first flight was not a success.

Everyone watched from the beach and the kookaburras tried very hard not to laugh, but when the harnessed kangaroos made their first attempt to pull the sleigh, it simply didn't move at all. Santa called out encouragement from his usual seat at the front of the sleigh. "On Donder! On Blitzen!" he called out, which is what he used to call out to his reindeer when they needed a bit of encouragement. But this had little effect. First, because the kangaroos had never really accepted their new reindeer names and secondly, even with Santa Claus himself calling encouragement from the Christmas sleigh, getting the thing up into the air and moving was a lot more work than kangaroos are used to.

But they didn't give up. They tried again, and then again. They rested, and then they tried again and again, and Santa called out encouragement, and the small crowd of Beachsiders called out encouragement and the kookaburras and parrots fluttered around making encouraging sounds and finally, after many failed attempts, when all the kangaroos tried very, very hard all together, the sleigh began to move. The trick, they discovered, was hopping all at the same time and pulling as hard as they possibly could. They got used to the idea and tried and tried, and eventually the sleigh began to move.

"Hurray!" shouted the little crowd on the beach. "Excellent work," said Santa. "Excellent."

The sleigh began to move slowly across the sand. It picked up speed little by little and the kangaroos began to understand how these things were done. They hopped faster and faster and pulled harder and harder and then, almost like a miracle, the giant sleigh, with Santa in the driver's seat, began to lift off the beach and into the bright blue Australian sky. The crowd cheered again, the kangaroos hopped and hopped and pulled and pulled and Santa's sleigh was airborne, just as it had to be on Christmas night.

You couldn't say it was a graceful flight. The sleigh lurched and bounced and Santa was bumped around quite badly in his seat, because no matter how many nice things you can say about kangaroos, they do not stride gracefully like reindeer when they are pulling a Christmas sleigh. They hop, as they were born to do, and hopping, instead of striding, does not make for a smooth ride in a Christmas sleigh. But they were doing the best they could.

Suddenly, however, disaster struck. The kangaroos were so happy they had managed to get the sleigh off the ground and so proud of themselves that they started acting a bit more like kangaroos again and forgot that this sort of work required a considerable amount of concentration. They started twitching their noses at each other and making soft little satisfied kangaroos sounds, and they looked down at their friends on the beach far below and then some of them started to realize exactly what they were doing and some of them forgot to hop in time with the other kangaroos in the team and things started, as adults often say, "to deteriorate badly".

The sleigh slowed down. It lost altitude, it became harder and harder to pull as it slowed and despite Santa's shouting of orders from the driver's seat, things started to look very bad indeed. The crowd on the beach gasped. The sleigh started to sway and circle and flap. Kookaburras and parrots rushed in formation to the scene but there was nothing they could do to help. Suddenly, the sleigh, the kangaroos, their harness and the fat old man in a red suit in the driver's seat crashed with a mighty splash, a fantastically big wet splash, into the waves.

The sleigh went in first, with its runners dragging dangerously on the waves for a minute while the kangaroos hopped like they had never hopped before, trying to stop it from crashing into the water. Then the sleigh itself went in, sending Santa over the side and into the water with a big fat splash. Then the kangaroos went in one by one by one, each making small kangaroo splashes and kangaroo spluttering and gasping noises as they went. It was all a truly awesome sight. In fact the crash of Santa's Christmas sleigh in the waves off Beachside, Australia, was the most amazing thing to happen to that little community ever. The crowd couldn't believe what it had seen.

At first they just stood there on the beach — elves, local friends, platypuses, and other Aussie animals. And of course, Mrs. Claus, who had watched the drama unfold in stunned silence. The tangle of kangaroos and leather harnesses made loud splashing sounds from out on the water. Santa, never a very strong swimmer at the best of times, tried his best to float but his heavy red Santa suit made things difficult. The sleigh itself had gone right out of sight but then suddenly, for reasons probably to do with its clever and secret design, bobbed up onto the surface like a gigantic bathtub toy. That was some small consolation.

Well, there is a lot more story to tell today, a lot more ground to cover, so I won't give you too many details here of the rescue. We have to get on to the next important part of the story. Let's just say that everyone on the beach rushed out to help the kangaroos and to help Santa. Some jumped into small boats and others swam right out. Some flew out and fluttered around giving what adults call "moral support". Let's just say it was a magnificent team effort and the whole thing turned out all right. The sleigh was towed back in to shore. The kangaroos were disentangled from their harnesses and pulled back onto shore. Santa was hoisted up onto a lifesaver's boat and hauled back onto shore. Everything turned out alright.

The crash victims sat on the beach catching their breath and resting. Mrs. Claus brought blankets, which is apparently what you are supposed to do after an incident of this sort, and everyone involved in the crash wrapped the blankets around their shoulders despite the heat and sat looking suitably dejected and wet. No one wanted to say to Mrs. Claus that in the hot Australian weather emergency blankets were not required. Most of the victims felt that blankets gave the scene an appropriately emergency look, so they all huddled under their blankets for a while, looking suitably dejected and wet.

But no one was hurt and for the kangaroos it had actually all been a wonderfully exhilarating adventure, to have flown into the air pulling Santa's Christmas sleigh and then to have crashed with a mighty splash into the ocean waves with a crowd of anxious friends watching the whole thing. Some of the kangaroos thought, in fact, that they might like to do it again, or maybe two or three times. But they didn't say that, because kangaroos are really quite silent types.

Anyway, that was when they were just learning. Soon, after they had rested for a few days and recuperated and got back their nerve, and under Santa's expert supervision, they got the hang of it quite nicely. Soon they were able to quite gracefully — not very gracefully, but quite gracefully — start hopping on the beach all together to get the sleigh moving, slowly at first, then faster and faster across the sand. Soon they were able to get the sleigh up into the sky quite regularly and soon they were able to pull it through the air without jolting and bumping Santa around too much.

Soon they were able to pull heavier and heavier loads, as they would have to do on Christmas Eve when the sleigh was full of toys. Santa ordered heavier and heavier loads to be placed in the back of the sleigh, to give the kangaroos practice and to get them into the best possible physical condition for the trip.

Soon Santa started attaching a sort of trailer to the back as well, because the plan was for Santa to bring as many helpers and friends and local animals along with him to the North Pole for the eventual big confrontation there. It was not going to be an easy thing for them to do, but they would fly to the North Pole, all together and relying on the element of surprise, take over the workshop and the surrounding area, throw out the people in suits and their mean helpers, retrieve all of the discarded letters from children all over the world, read all of the letters carefully, make all of the toys that had been requested, and deliver these on time and in good condition all around the world on Christmas Eve.

It was, as adults would probably say, a "very tall order". No one thought it was going to be easy, but this was Santa's plan and he was in charge of Christmas and they were all in this together and they were determined to make it work.

They didn't have much time and there was a lot more to do to get ready. While Santa and the kangaroos practiced every day flying over the beach in the Christmas sleigh, Mrs. Claus saw to other urgent matters. It would be true to say that Mrs. Claus was what adults would call "a details person". She looked after a lot of the practical details of any adventure, while Santa was, well, if not a visionary then a man who looked at what adults call "the big picture". Which means that he often forgot important things like proper clothing for an adventure, or sandwiches, or weather forecasts, or maps, or the proper authorization documents and licenses and official papers. That sort of thing. So Mrs. Claus saw to the details, while Santa practiced flying with his kangaroos.

It was going to be a big crowd of people and animals in the sleigh when they eventually took off for the North Pole and Mrs. Claus wanted to make sure everything was ready for the long flight. She assigned elves to make boxed lunches, for example, and she assigned some of the local people to knit woolly hats and caps and scarves for everyone who was not used to the cold. Making woolly hats and caps and scarves for people is not an easy thing to do at the best of times. But to make odd-shaped woolly items for kookaburras and platypuses and kangaroos is quite another. So Mrs. Claus had a lot of work and worrying to do. She wanted to make sure everything was ready and that all would be done on time.

Well, everything was ready, eventually. There were some last minute hitches and problems and setbacks along the way, but everyone worked very

hard and very long and eventually everything was ready. The kangaroos had got quite good at pulling the sleigh. Santa had got better at driving a team of kangaroos, as opposed to team of reindeer. Mrs. Claus and her helpers had done an excellent job of seeing to the details and so, eventually, one cloudy Australian night, they were all ready to go.

They had chosen a cloudy night because they didn't want to draw too much attention to themselves when they took off. It's true that the plan to fly to the North Pole and save Christmas was pretty much of an open secret around Beachside. But not many other people in Australia, or anywhere else in the world for that matter, knew about the plan, and Santa wanted to keep it that way. So he decided they would wait for one of Australia's rare cloudy days and take off that night if the cloud stayed around.

The clouds, as hoped, did stay around. Everyone assembled on the beach, according to plan, and everyone looked very serious. Some of them even looked a little worried. Because it is one thing to make a plan and practice on a beach and talk about what you are going to do. It is quite another thing, when the time actually comes, to begin an adventure. That is when you start to realize what you have got yourself into and what may or may not happen next. That is when people start to get slightly worried looks on their faces and talk quietly amongst themselves and try not to be the first one to say something negative about the whole idea. No one wanted to admit it, but they knew this was going to be a very big adventure, and no one quite knew how it was all going to turn out. All they knew was that they had agreed to do it and so they simply had no choice but to go ahead and do it.

Santa climbed up into the driver's seat of the sleigh. Mrs. Claus climbed up beside him. Piles of sacks and boxes of supplies and adventure equipment sat in the back behind them. The trailer full of locals and local animals and friends was attached to the back of the sleigh. Platypuses squeezed into seats beside Beachsiders. Koala bears sat squeezed in beside kookaburras. Parrots fluttered and squawked alongside. Everyone was bundled up with woolly hats and caps and scarves. It was all a wonderfully exotic sight.

The kangaroos got into position. They, too, looked wonderfully exotic in their new hats and scarves. They looked nervous but determined. Santa himself looked nervous but determined. He had on a freshly laundered and pressed Santa suit and he had combed his big white beard and waxed his moustaches and done everything he could to make himself look like the official and only Santa Claus, the man in charge of Christmas. He looked around at his team of friends and helpers, and he raised his hand and shouted out: "This is it, friends and colleagues. Best of luck to one and all. We are off to save Christmas!"

With that he gave the sign and the team of kangaroos hopped and pulled for all they were worth and the sleigh and trailer began to move slowly across the sand. It moved faster and faster and faster and then, suddenly, it was airborne. Everyone gave a big gasp of surprise and excitement and the sleigh arched up as gracefully as possible under the circumstances and went high, high and higher into the night sky. It got smaller and smaller and smaller and then, all of a sudden, it disappeared behind a giant cloud. The adventure had begun. Santa was on his way back to the North Pole.

Well, the story is really moving along quickly now. We are getting to the end, or at least nearer to the end, now. Santa is on his way to the North Pole to save Christmas, after weeks and weeks of planning and preparation. The people in suits and their mean helpers are working away up there, probably without a clue as to what is coming their way. Probably. You can never tell, of course. And we are sitting here wondering what is going to happen next and it won't be long now until we find out. But, as usual, I have to warn any of you out there who find adventure stories like this, important adventure stories like this, to be scary or distressing that you'll have to hang on tight. Because you can't come to the end of a story like this just like that. You've got to have more twists and turns along the way and you really never know just how a story like this is going to turn out.

The flight of Santa's Christmas sleigh from Beachside, Australia, to the North Pole was as uneventful as a flight like that could ever be. Santa took the sleigh up as high as he could, as high as the kangaroos could manage, given how little experience they had and how unaccustomed they were to cold night air. They were working hard and doing an excellent job. They hopped all together, mostly, and the ride for Santa and everyone in the back was as smooth as they could possibly make it. But, as we know, hopping like a kangaroos is not the same as striding like a reindeer, especially an experienced Christmas sleigh reindeer, so there were, to be perfectly frank, a fair number of bumps and jolts along the way.

The cold, in fact, was the worst problem for most of the Aussie people and animals and birds on the flight. Even though they had woolly things to wear, most of the Aussies felt the cold. Little icicles, in fact, formed on the noses of the kangaroos and the platypuses and the koalas. The kookaburras had to flap their wings very, very fast, not just to keep up with Santa but the keep their wings themselves from icing up, a common problem in cold weather aviation.

As for Santa, well, he was simply determined to get everyone there as soon as he possibly could. The truth of the matter is he looked a little grim as he sat in the driver's seat next to Mrs. Claus, trying to find his way to the North Pole in the cold and the dark. He peered determinedly straight ahead, with ice forming on his beard and eyebrows, trying to find the fastest way possible so that all of his friends and helpers wouldn't suffer too much in the cold. Mrs. Claus sat next to him, looking remarkably calm. She was well bundled, and really all you could see was her very red checks and shiny dark eyes and the tip of her Mrs. Claus nose.

It was a long night, and a long flight. As they drew nearer to the North Pole, somewhere after the frozen wastes of Canada, Santa called out to everyone in a loud, firm voice that they had better eat some sandwiches, because no one could be sure when they might have a chance to eat next.

The kangaroos looked at each other somewhat nervously at this, but they kept on hopping as fast as they could. No one had thought about how they might be able to eat sandwiches as they flew, so they wondered when they would get to eat for the first time, let alone the next time. Santa seemed to think they could fly all the way to the North Pole on nearly empty stomachs. But they didn't give up.

The elves scurried around as best they could in the sleigh and in the trailer, serving sandwiches and hot chocolate from steaming silver flasks. It was cozy enough, eating sandwiches and sipping hot chocolate way up high over the world in the cold dark air. It seemed, in a way, like some very strange picnic. It was certainly an adventure, and everyone knows adventures are best when sandwiches and hot chocolate are available.

When everyone had finished eating, they noticed that the sun was rising, pink and gold, on the wintry horizon. Santa's face suddenly had that doubly wrinkled expression we know about, the expression he put on when things were not quite right. For you see, he had hoped to arrive at the North Pole under what adults call "the cover of darkness". This, he had hoped, would allow him to use all of his extensive Santa Claus flight training to swoop in low and fast over the workshops and barns and, using the element of surprise, take back what was rightfully his without too much of a bother.

He worried now, however, that if the sun came up and things got too bright, that the people in suits and their guards and supervisors would see them in the air and take some kind of defensive action. He shuddered to think what that might be.

"On Dasher! On Dancer!" he called out to the kangaroos with a worried sideways look at Mrs. Claus. "We haven't a moment to lose," he said. The kangaroos hopped faster and faster, as fast as they could given the circumstances and the fact that they had not had any sandwiches or hot chocolate to give them extra strength. They hopped as fast as they could and the sleigh surged ahead. For the passengers, it was all quite exhilarating. For the kangaroos, it was simply hard work.

Suddenly Mrs. Claus called out: "There it is! There it is! We've made it back to the North Pole!" Everyone strained to get a better look, particularly the Australians, none of whom had even seen snow before, let alone the North Pole. "Fair dinkum?" said one of the Beachsiders, the one who used to wear the big old sun hat and the baggiest shorts. He wasn't wearing beach gear now and you could hardly see his face for the woolly hat and the giant scarf he had wound around and around his sunburned neck. "Stone the crows! It's the North Pole!"

Now some of you might think the North Pole would actually be a big pole stuck somewhere in the snow somewhere north of Canada, and easy to spot. That is not the case. In fact, the exact location of the North Pole is in some dispute. What Mrs. Claus was referring to was the big group of buildings and barns and workshops and walls that formed Santa's North Pole workshop. There was no pole, but it was clear something important had been built down there on the ice and snow, and that it had been there for a long time. There was not another sign of life anywhere in any direction. Just the toy workshops and living quarters.

Santa knew he had to hurry before it got too light. Smoke and steam were rising from chimneys below and he knew that his elves and their new bosses were getting breakfast, getting ready for another day making toys and throwing away important letters from boys and girls all over the world. The thought of those discarded letters made his face even redder than usual and deepened his deepest wrinkles. Santa circled the workshop area, hoping against hope they would not be seen. He hoped the guards were busy with their breakfasts. He brought the sleigh down lower, very fast, and everyone gasped and looked at each other in alarm.

You can imagine how scary all of this was for everyone on board. But they were brave, and determined, which is how you have to be on an adventure of this sort. They all peered over the sides of the sleigh and the trailer and waited for Santa to make his final move. Santa couldn't see any sign of life on the snow outside the buildings. He knew he had only a few minutes before someone came out and spotted the giant sleigh. So he knew what he had to do.

"Assume the brace position!" he called out. "Seat trays in the upright position!" Everyone put their heads up against the person in front of them and generally got ready for a bumpy landing. "Kangas!" Santa bellowed. "Prepare for landing!" The kangaroos were prepared to be prepared, but as they had never actually landed on anything other than water or sand before they weren't quite sure what to do. They just put their noses in the air and tried to look as professional as possible. They were as ready as they ever could be. Scared, but ready, which is about right for an adventure.

"Hold very tight!" Santa cried. "We're going in. Good luck to everyone!" That was supposed to reassure everyone but, as you can imagine, it did not. In fact, it made a few of the nervous fliers even more nervous than they already were. But no one said a word.

Santa banked the sleigh hard to the right, then to the left, then to the right again, trying to come in at exactly the correct angle for a smooth landing on a clear space outside the main workshop. The kangaroo were getting dizzy with all the changes in direction. Their noses twitched and they made breathless little kangaroos sounds as they hopped. This was the moment of truth, the moment they had all been in training for so many weeks. They hoped they would be able to

perform. The very future of Christmas was in their paws.

Santa bellowed out orders. "Pull up. Left! Left! Left! Pull up! Smooth out! Watch your altitude! Watch my altitude! Watch everyone's altitude!"

It was not the sort of elegant landing that you might have expected had reindeers been pulling the sleigh. I think it is fair to say that. Reindeers, when they are pulling a fully laden Christmas sleigh are experts at gliding in somewhere, bringing the sleigh and all its contents in for a very smooth and elegant landing. Little puffs of snow waft up from the sleigh runners, the sleigh glides smoothly forward onto the snow and it slows down nicely and Santa climbs off in a very dignified fashion, waving and going "Ho! Ho! Ho!" as everyone expects him to do.

The kangaroo landing was not like that at all. As the sleigh came in very close to the ground, a few of the kangaroos started to get alarmed. One of them, we won't say which one, started to try to pull up again, if only because the sight of all that snow was something he had never seen before. This particular kangaroo, who we will not name, wasn't sure he liked the idea of putting his paws down in what everyone had said would be a freezing North Pole equivalent of beach sand. Mrs. Claus had arranged for everyone to have woolly hats and scarves and caps, but she had not thought about boots, or perhaps had thought boots would not be necessary for kangaroos.

So this one kangaroo, with a sudden fear of snow — really, we shouldn't name him, particularly as naming him would draw unfair attention to his red nose — created what you might call a chain reaction. He tried to pull up while everyone else was going down. This was not a good thing. It confused everyone and made it hard for Santa to steer. Some of the other kangaroos near the front starting to get tangled in their harnesses. A couple stumbled and stopped hopping. The others had trouble hopping together. The sleigh bobbed and swayed alarmingly. Santa and Mrs. Claus looked ahead of them with triply wrinkled looks on their faces. The passengers all cried out in fright. It did not look very promising at all.

The whole lot of them came tumbling down onto the snow at great speed, a huge tangle of kangaroos, harnesses, Santa suit, elves, hot chocolate flasks, adventure equipment, woolly hats and caps and scarves. It was just a huge, snowy tumble of people, animals and gear of all sorts, tumbling and tumbling over and over in the fluffy white snow. The kangaroos gasped and struggled in their harnesses. Santa went for a somersault off to the side and landed flat on his back. Mrs. Claus managed to hang on to her seat. The kookaburras and parrots, the lucky ones, soared up and away from the crash scene. Everyone else lay in a jumble in the sleigh, in the trailer and on the snow. It was not a pretty sight.

But no one was hurt. The sleigh lay on its side in the snow but it appeared not to have been damaged. No one said anything for a few seconds and then Santa called out, in a small voice from where he lay: "That is not quite how it is supposed to be."

The kangaroos felt sad and embarrassed. But they knew they had done the best they could and they knew Santa knew that too. So they struggled to get out of their harnesses and the others picked themselves up and dusted the snow from their clothes and faces. Elves rushed to help Santa get up, and others helped Mrs. Claus. Everyone was OK.

But the accident had distracted them. It took them a while to realize that the crash, while it didn't make much noise in the deep snow, was certainly very hard to miss. A crowd of guards rushed out from the breakfast hall and gathered around the accident scene. They were "flabbergasted" at what they saw, which is a word you use when you are very, very, very surprised. One of them ran as fast as he could to call the supervisors. One to get the people in suits. You could see right away that this was going to be a very tense stand-off.

Santa Claus, still out of breath from the crash and still pretty much covered in snow, stood up as straight as he could and said to the flabbergasted guards: "I'm back!" Mrs. Claus came over to his side: "Me too!" she said. The others all crowded over to where Santa stood. "We're back!" they all said, which was not strictly true, as some of them had never set foot in the place before. But in an adventure of this sort, things occasionally get said which are not strictly true. "We're back!" everyone said in loud, strong voices.

The guards looked very scared and worried. They had taken on their jobs thinking there would never be any trouble. The guards' job descriptions in fact had stipulated that they would generally just have to oversee toy-making activities and make sure that elves did not sing or write letters and that they took only half an hour to eat their triangle sandwiches at lunch time. Some of the guards, in fact, thought the job was the easiest thing imaginable.

But this situation, facing down an angry crowd of Santa supporters, was not going to be easy. The guards realized that right away. They looked at each other nervously as they waited for their supervisors to come. They were not sure what they should do next. One of them actually looked for the relevant section in his job description booklet but could find nothing that covered this sort of thing. It was, as everyone hearing this story for the first time might have expected, a very tense stand-off.

Well, these situations sometimes have a way of resolving themselves very quickly. Because, you see, none of the guards and probably even none, or not many, of the supervisors or the people in suits really wanted any serious trouble. When the supervisors and the people in suits came out and saw what was going on and saw that Santa Claus was back, and with a crowd of determined-looking friends, they knew that there was probably not much they could do. But at first they tried. They put on, as adults say, a "very brave face".

The bravest of the brave faces were on the most senior people in suits. They stood between the two opposing groups and said, all together, to Santa and his friends: "You people are trespassing.

We have a contractual arrangement. You are not welcome here. Please leave immediately. The guards will escort you out." The guards looked at each other nervously. This was not in their job description. The one with the job description booklet flipped furiously through the pages, looking for where it said they had to escort an angry crowd out of the workshop. He couldn't see where this was written down.

Santa said: "We're not going anywhere. We are here to stay. We are here to save Christmas!"

"Hurray!" shouted his crowd of friends. "Oh Santa, hurray!" said Mrs. Claus. She was very proud.

"Guards!" said the people in suits. "Please escort these people off the premises."

The guards didn't know what to do. They looked nervously at their supervisors, who were just as nervous. They all looked at the people in suits and they looked at the crowd of Santa supporters and they didn't know what to do at all.

Well, sometimes in these circumstances

something happens that answers everybody's questions for them. In this case, it came from the back of the crowd of Santa supporters. It was a big, perfectly-formed snowball. It sailed up from the back of Santa's crowd and over their heads and landed with a satisfying "Thump!" right in the ear of the tallest of the people in suits. Then another snowball whizzed out from the back of Santa's crowd. Then another, and another. These were high-velocity snowballs, perfectly round and soft and squishy and they landed with a series of "thump, thump, thumpetty thump" sounds on the people in suits, and on the guards.

No one knew who had actually cast the first snowball. Some said afterward it was one of the Beachsiders, but few believed that story. Australians have limited experience of snowballs and snowball fights, even though they are fast learners and great companions when the going gets tough. Someone else said it was one of the elves who fired the first snowball and many others thought this was probably true. Elves at the North

Pole know a lot about snow and snowballs and snowball fights, so it is quite likely that one of the elves fired that first important shot.

No matter who came up with the idea and who fired the first snowball, it started a ferocious battle in the snow. Snowballs whizzed back and forth across the front line. Snowballs landed with heavy thumps on everyone. Snowballs positively rained down from all directions. The people in suits did their best, but, by definition, people in suits are not accustomed to having ferocious snowball fights with anyone, let alone with a crowd of Santa supporters at the North Pole.

People started rolling in the snow as they struggled for advantage. Everyone got completely covered in snow and soaked and out of breath, which is exactly what is supposed to happen in a good, fair snowball fight. Everyone was covered in snow and all were making snowballs just as fast as they could and the battle raged for some minutes before it was clear who was going to win.

Well, of course Santa's side won. He had the

strength of numbers. And his side had occupied what adults would call "the moral high ground". They also had air support, from the parrots and kookaburras, who whizzed in and out of the battleground dropping small but effective snowballs directly onto people's heads from high above. The guards, for their part, did not have their hearts in the snowball battle anyway, nor did their supervisors. The people in suits were not good snowball battlers at all, having relied too long on others to fight their snowball battles for them.

And the fact of the matter is no one wanted to hurt anyone else and no one really wanted to fight over any of this at all anyway. So the people in suits eventually sat down with a series of soft bumps on the snow and cried out: "Enough! Enough! Enough!"

Santa's crowd cheered and clapped. "Enough! Enough! They've had enough!" they all shouted, laughing and shaking each other's hands.

Santa looked very proud. He gave Mrs. Claus

a very big North Pole style hug. He rushed around shaking hands with all of his friends and helpers and he patted each of the kangaroos on their heads one by one. Then his smile disappeared.

He advanced menacingly to the crowd of guards and supervisors and people in suits who had all sat down in the trampled snow where the epic snowball battle had taken place. No one knew what he was going to do or say. Everyone grew silent. They waited while Santa stared at the guards and supervisors and people in suits for a very long time. His face was very red. He had triple wrinkles and a very stern expression. He stared and stared and he huffed and puffed like a big toy steam engine. Eventually he spoke.

"This has been positively preposterous!" Santa said grimly. "All of this!"

The guards and the supervisors and the people in suits stared in silence at the snow-covered ground. The truth of the matter is that they knew Santa was right. They were all a little ashamed of themselves, if the truth were known.

But they said nothing. They just stared at the ground and waited to see what Santa was going to do with them.

"You have all put Christmas as we know it in grave danger," Santa said. "Very grave danger." When Santa was in a serious mood, or angry, he tended to repeat things a little, for effect. It gave him what grown-ups call "leadership quality".

He paused, and looked all around, at the workshops and his crowd of friends and at the huddled group of frightened guards, supervisors and people in suits.

"I'm afraid you have left me no choice," he said gravely. Everyone grew very still and silent. They had no idea what horrible punishment Santa was going to dish out.

"I'm afraid that I'm going to have to insist," he said, "that each and every one of you stay here and help make things right. I order all of you to work as fast and as hard as you possibly can alongside my friends here to make things right for Christmas. That means hours and hours and days and days of hard work. I'm afraid you have no choice. Christmas is coming very, very soon and we have very little time."

The crowd of Santa supporters cheered. "Hurray!" they all cried out. "They will help us make things right!"

The guards and supervisors and people in suits looked a little bit relieved. But they still said nothing.

"However," Santa said, and the crowd went silent again. "However, as further punishment, I am going to have to insist that you eat nothing but triangle sandwiches for your lunch and dinner, until all of those horrible sandwiches are gone forever."

The crowd gasped. This was harsh punishment, very harsh indeed.

The guards and supervisors and people in suits looked pretty unhappy with this last bit of news. But they said nothing right away. They just started to look up one by one, and then at each other and then at Santa's crowd. Eventually the most senior people in suits said, all together, which is how they seemed to talk: "All right, Santa. Yes, all right. We're ever so sorry for all of this and we will help make things right."

That sent a huge cheer up from the crowd, and Santa's crowd all rushed over and embraced and shook hands with their new friends and colleagues. Everyone brightened up immensely. It became almost like a party in the snow. The kangaroos hopped around happily. The reindeer waved their antlers back and forth. Mrs. Claus wiped a tear from her eye. Santa stood back watching it all from a distance, and quickly wiped a tear away from his eye, too. It looked like everything was going to turn out right.

But there was an enormous amount of work to do. They decided to start immediately. Santa made lots of lists and gave people assignments. Mrs. Claus got busy with her favorite elves to see what else needed to be done. Others went out back to retrieve the discarded letters from boys and girls all over the world, and began sorting and reading them and making lists. Santa checked out the workshops. And soon that workshop was full of the sound of elfin hammers tapping and little saws sawing and the happy sound of singing as people worked.

One of the more delicate problems, of course, was reindeer-kangaroo relations. Santa knew this wasn't going to be easy. The reindeer had been left behind at the North Pole while Santa lived in Australia, and you could say that some of them were quite unhappy when they learned that he had recruited a team of eight kangaroos to, essentially, take their place. Santa knew he would have to use all of his diplomatic skills to smooth over this problem. Especially when he told the reindeer he had given their names to the eight kangaroos.

At first the reindeer were a bit cold, which is not too unusual really, given that reindeer have spent all of their lives in the frozen North Pole. But they were particularly cold in a sort of social sense when they were introduced to the kangaroos. They were not happy when Santa explained how he had trained them to pull the sleigh and how hard they had all worked to get everyone safely back to the North Pole. But Santa was good at this sort of thing and he took a few key reindeer aside and whispered things into their ears and they slowly began to understand that he had really had no choice.

Then, when the reindeer had spent a little bit of time with the kangaroos and got to know them, they started to come around nicely. Rudolph the red nosed reindeer hit it off particularly well with Rudolph the red-nosed kangaroo, for obvious reasons. That seemed to break the ice and eventually the reindeer and kangaroos were making quiet little noises amongst themselves and exchanging notes on aerodynamics and other important matters. Because Santa had explained to them that on Christmas Eve they would all be flying together, in an unprecedented international team of reindeer and kangaroos and using a special harness. This would allow them to pull the exceptionally heavy sleigh at exceptionally high speeds. Because this was going to be a very special and important Christmas, a sort of emergency Christmas, and Santa was going to do everything he could to make it go right.

They all worked as hard as they possibly could. All of the children's letters got read, and all of the lists of presents were amended and brought up to date. The elves worked night and day on their toy making. The reindeer and kangaroos spent long hours practicing how to pull a Christmas sleigh together with a special harness, not an easy task because, as you know by now, reindeers stride when they pull a sleigh and kangaroos hop. But they worked very hard and took many practice runs, with Santa in the driver's seat and after a few mishaps and, yes, even a few crashes into the snow, everyone got the hang of it and they were able to pull the sleigh in a sort of hop-hop, glide-glide sort of way which, while not terribly smooth and comfortable for Santa, did eventually work reasonably well.

No one seemed to mind all of the hard work. Even the guards and supervisors and people in suits worked very hard. They, in fact, quite quickly "redeemed themselves", which is what adults say when people act horribly for a while and then suddenly act wonderfully and helpfully and make everyone think they are OK after all. Once that happened, Santa felt badly about insisting that they eat nothing but triangle sandwiches for lunch and dinner, so he invited them to join in the fun of the regular North Pole lunch, where everyone ate hot and tasty things and sang songs and told stories while they ate.

All of the bad things were, in fact, soon forgotten. There was just too much work to do to dwell on bad things that had gone on in the past.

Well, we're getting pretty close to the end of the story now, as you have probably already guessed. That is the thing about stories like this. You go through a lot of adventures and a lot of ups and downs and you really don't know at all how things are going to turn out. Then, suddenly, the story turns and starts heading toward the end and you get a pretty good idea of where it's going to end up. And this story, as with all good Christmas stories, always, ends up on Christmas Eve.

You can imagine how hard it was for everyone to get everything ready for the big night. All the letters, every single one, had to be read and considered and responded to. All of the toy orders had to be filled, despite the delays and the wasted time caused by the hostile takeover of Santa's workshop by the people in suits. Then the reindeer and kangaroos had to be trained and trained and trained and prepared for their big challenge. Santa Claus and Mrs. Claus had to see to getting all of the food and supplies ready for the big flight of the Christmas sleigh. All of the elves and helpers and new friends had to be trained and prepared and equipped with their proper woolly clothes and hats and so on and so forth. You have already got a pretty good idea of what a big job all of that was.

But by late in the afternoon on Christmas Eve, North Pole time, everyone was ready. Everything was in place, everyone knew what had to be done.

The reindeer and kangaroos were hitched up in their special leather harness, which would allow them to pull the sleigh all together. The sleigh and the trailer were packed incredibly high with toys of all sorts; toys in sacks, toys in stacks, toys in the back. Then all of the passengers and supporters piled on. The airborne regiment — that is, the kookaburras and the magpies and the parrots — hovered around in formation waiting for the big moment when the sleigh would take off on its round-the-world journey to deliver toys to all good little girls and boys. Eventually, everything was absolutely, positively, well and truly ready.

Then Santa came out. He was smiling from ear to ear, a very wide smile in a man so big as he. He looked splendid in a freshly cleaned and pressed Santa suit, the best one he owned. Mrs. Claus looked a picture too, in her matching Mrs.

Claus suit. Everyone looked just right.

All that remained was to get that giant sleigh, laden as it was never laden before with toys and friends and helpers, off into the sky and on its way. No one wanted to be the first to admit they were a little bit worried about whether the international kangaroo-reindeer team could do the job. No one wants to be the first to admit worrying, but there were definitely a few worried faces in the crowd.

Time was getting on and there were no other jobs to finish or problems to solve. It was time to get the sleigh on its way. It was getting late, the sun was going down and little boys and girls all over the world were getting into their beds, depending on the time zone, and getting ready to sleep so that they could wake up as soon as possible and open their presents.

Santa took one last walk around his sleigh and his international kangaroo-reindeer team. He looked everything over one last time and then he climbed aboard alongside Mrs. Claus. He adjusted his scarves. He adjusted the reins of the new harness. He looked this way and that. And, when there was no longer any possible reason for further delay, he called out in his heartiest Santa Claus voice: "This is it, my friends! This is it! Let's get on with it, right now!"

He cried out again to his waiting transport team with the words they had all agreed would be fair and accurate, given the fact that this year they were 16 in number instead of the usual eight, and sharing names. "On Comet Comet! On Blitzen Blitzen! On Donder Donder! Up, up and away!"

With that the kangaroos and reindeer began to pull the sleigh slowly forward. Torches burned orange beside the runway in the failing North Pole light. The sleigh inched ahead, slowly, slowly, slowly at first, then ever so slightly faster, then faster and faster and faster and faster. The runners kicked up little puffs of soft white snow. The crowd of people on board pulled down their woolly caps and leaned forward in excitement, as if to help the team pull their heavy load. The whole contraption — sleigh, trailer, toys, passengers, everything — all began to move steadily toward the tall evergreen trees at the end of the North Pole runway.

The kangaroos hopped as fast as they could. The reindeer strode and strode as fast as they could, trying to glide but hampered a little, as they knew they would be, by the hops of the kangaroos. They all pulled and hopped and strode as hard as they possibly could. The sleigh rose slightly off the snow, then bounced down with a little bump, then two bumps, then three. Then it raised again off the snow, with everyone gasping, and clasping each other and leaning forward as far as they could in their seats. The evergreen trees at the end of the runway loomed bigger and bigger and bigger. The kangaroos hopped harder. The reindeer strode faster.

Santa called out again and again: "On Cupid Cupid! On Prancer Prancer! Up, up and away!"

Then, suddenly, with just seconds to spare, the sleigh got truly airborne. It lurched to and fro, left and right, up and down as the team really started to get it going. It almost hit the evergreen tress, which would have been a disaster, but missed them by a whisker. Santa lurched into Mrs. Claus. Passengers lurched into each other in the back. The sacks of toys lurched alarmingly, with their precious cargo all but falling over the side. But then the kangaroos and the reindeer got into their stride, got the hopping under control, got the entire amazing contraption under control, and they were away.

Well, the place to have been at that very moment, as you can imagine, would have been back down on the North Pole runway, looking up into the late evening sky. The last shafts of golden sunlight were disappearing. The sky was just going from pink to purple to blue to blue-black inky blue. The moon was coming up over the horizon, as it would on such an important night. If you had been on the North Pole runway at the very moment you would have seen a sight you could never forget.

Santa's sleigh and his trailer and his gigantic

load of friends and helpers and toys and equipment and supplies, arched up higher and higher and faster and faster and directly in front of the wonderfully round and friendly moon and then you could see the whole amazing sight silhouetted beautifully, just for an instant, before it whooshed higher and higher and, eventually, out of sight.

Well, the rest, as adults sometimes say, is history. Santa and his friends did exactly what they had to do that night, and did it just right. All the toys got delivered, there were no mishaps, no major mishaps. All the good little boys and girls got the lovely well-made toys they had wished for so hard, and all of the mothers and fathers breathed big sighs of relief on Christmas morning. Santa Claus and Mrs. Claus hugged each other and tears formed in their ancient eyes as they finished their long night's work, knowing that against all odds Christmas had been saved.

The passengers on that sleigh that night all had wonderful stories to tell their grandchildren.

Their grandchildren would have the whole story to tell their own grandchildren, and now you, too, will have this story to tell, to anybody you like, anywhere, any Christmas, anytime. Just remember who told you this story for the first time, and how you felt about it then, and try very hard to make that feeling come back each time you hear it or tell it or tell it again. The story, the once-secret story, of the Kangaroo Christmas.